A Diamond In The Rough

TWO SISTERS

By : Bobbie Gambrell

Illustrated by
Arsalan

iUniverse books may be ordered through booksellers or by contacting:

iUniverse
1663 Liberty Drive
Bloomington, IN 47403
www.iuniverse.com
844-349-9409

Because of the dynamic nature of the Internet, any web addresses or links contained in this book may have changed since publication and may no longer be valid. The views expressed in this work are solely those of the author and do not necessarily reflect the views of the publisher, and the publisher hereby disclaims any responsibility for them.

Any people depicted in stock imagery provided by Getty Images are models, and such images are being used for illustrative purposes only. Certain stock imagery © Getty Images.

ISBN: 978-1-6632-2723-2 (sc)
978-1-6632-2724-9 (e)

Library of Congress Control Number: 2021915660

Print information available on the last page.

iUniverse rev. date: 07/30/2021

A Diamond In The Rough

TWO SISTERS

Once upon a time, there were two little girls who lived in the woods with their mom.

Their father left when Latasha was very little. So one day they asked their mother if they could go play in the woods. She said yes, just don't go in the cave.

As soon as they went outside, Latasha saw a squirrel and started running behind it. Without thinking they ran deeper in the woods right into the cave.

Latesha called out to Latasha telling her to come back but she didn't listen, just like many little sisters. And just like a big sister Latesha ran into the cave behind her.

Once they got into the cave, they saw two big red eyes and to their surprise, it was a big black bear. He let out a big scary roar that scared the girls and they ran even deeper into the cave.

While running, they saw something shining. So Latasha ran over to the pile of dirt to see what it was. It was a big beautiful diamond. At that moment the same squirrel ran pass them and back out of the cave.

And like before, they ran after him and past the big black bear. Sitting like nothing ever happened was that pesky little squirrel eating a nut. Latasha ran toward the squirrel and he ran at the tree.

After that, the girls ran home in excitement to share with their mom what they had found. Standing on the porch when they finally reached home was their mom saying " I know y'all been in that cave." Latasha said yes ma'am, but look what we found! With unbelief in her eyes mama replied and said " I think this is the biggest diamond I ever seen." So are you still mad at us? Asked Latesha. I was never mad just worried that something may happen to you. I know I get busy at times and can't always watch, but I'm going to do better. That's why I'm thankful that you two have each other.

And on that day, they were able to move out of the woods and into the city. The family had all they ever wanted and needed which is each other. And they lived happily ever after.

CPSIA information can be obtained
at www.ICGtesting.com
Printed in the USA
BVHW022142121121
621467BV00002BA/23